AF388593

HIDDEN IN THE MARGINS

by Magali Elisa Moon

Bibliografische Information der Deutschen Nationalbibliothek: Die Deutsche Nationalbibliothek verzeichnet diese Publikation in der Deutschen Nationalbibliografie; detaillierte bibliografische Daten sind im Internet über dnb.dnb.de abrufbar.
Die automatisierte Analyse des Werkes, um daraus Informationen insbesondere über Muster, Trends und Korrelationen gemäß §44b UrhG („Text und Data Mining") zu gewinnen, ist untersagt.
© 2024 Magali Elisa Moon
Cover photo: Luna Magali Rothe
Verlag: BoD · Books on Demand GmbH, In de Tarpen 42, 22848 Norderstedt
Druck: Libri Plureos GmbH, Friedensallee 273, 22763 Hamburg
ISBN: 978-3-7583-5067-2

To all those who have been deemed weird and un-
usual, and to the resilient souls navigating loneliness, mental health battles and chronic illnesses - this
book is dedicated to your strength, uniqueness and
the courage to embrace your journey.
Your stories matter.

CONTENT

II

Chapter 1: the willows haven

Midway through my first year at college, I discovered the weeping willow tree at the edge of the campus, far away from the buzzing little English town filled with students. That's what I loved about it. It was quiet and lonely enough, so that I was able to be alone with my thoughts and read without any disturbance. I spent almost all my time there, at least the time that I was not spending in the beautiful ancient university library, watching the movement of the lake or reading one of my beloved library books.

It was another one of these cold rainy fall days and I decided to take a nice evening stroll to my tree. I was craving some space for my thoughts to breathe. The raindrops tapped a gentle rhythm on my umbrella as I walked with my dimly lit torch towards the willows haven. As I approached the edge of the campus, the sounds of the town began to fade and were replaced by a distant lull in the lake and the occasional wind whispering through the willows branches. I settled down onto the damp ground, not caring about my clothes getting wet and dirty.

I started to stare into the distance, lost in thought, before the worn pages of my library book found their way into my hands, and I escaped into the written words. With each page turned, the veil between reality and imagination faded more and more, and I felt myself almost becoming trapped in this reality that I wished was mine.

But just when things felt almost magical, reality hit me like a sudden jolt. The world around me snapped back into focus, and I was reminded that the escape that I desperately craved was only within the pages of a book.

I sat there on the cold stony ground, and realized that in the enchanting realms of literature, my mind could wander freely, yet the persistent throbbing of my limbs severed like an anchor to reality. A tear softly rolled down my cheek, as I watched the rain, mirroring the quiet ache within my soul.

My thoughts started to wonder, and I questioned my whole existence again, and why it always had to be me.

"With what had I deserved this?! I must have been an awful person in my last life. There is no other explanation, or maybe I am an awful person in this life and I just don't know it yet..."

I started to shiver, and then I realized that it was getting darker and colder with every minute passing by. My drenched clothes stuck to my body, and I decided that it was time to get back before I caught a cold.

As I walked down the cobblestone path that led to my dormitory, goosebumps spread across my skin. I opened the door, water dripping from my jacket and, without hesitating, I made my way to the showers. The water became a comforting embrace, washing away the weariness clinging to me. The water was so hot, it almost felt like it would burn my skin away, but I did not mind that feeling.

Emerging from the shower with my wet hair wrapped in a towel, I made my way to my dorm room. And as soon as I reached my bed, I collapsed onto it. I stared at my ceiling for a couple of minutes before I turned onto my side and glared into the stars instead. I settled against the pillows, the stars twinkled, distant yet comforting, each one holding a story untold.

It was a clear night, it had stopped raining a while ago, and the moon was in its full glory. The quiet of the room was broken only by the soft humming of the radiator and the occasional rustle of leaves dancing in the night breeze in front of my window. My eyes got heavier and heavier with each breath that I took, and after a little while I drifted into the deep darkness of my dreams.

Chapter 2: halls of fatigue

My head was throbbing again, just like it had done the past couple of days. The class dragged on and on, and it felt like an endless stretch of monotony. I stared at the ticking clock, desperately counting down the seemingly eternal 20 minutes. The old lecture hall, with its stone walls and neatly arranged antique wooden desks, felt suffocating and like it was closing in on me. Lost in my thoughts, I reached for my water bottle, which was tucked away in the corner of my bag. Everything had started to spin. The world swirled around me, and the voice of professor Williams started to blend in with the hum of the lights. I released my greasy dark hair from my bun, feeling an immediate release of tension.

As the bell finally rang, I packed my things in a rush, realizing I had forgotten to take any notes, but at that moment I did not care, all I wanted to do was to get out of this stuffy room.

I made my way through the dimly lit hallways, the old wooden floors betraying the passage of countless students. My upper lip curled as a jumble of different human scents wafted through the air, the overwhelming mixture stirring a wave of disgust within me.

As soon as I reached the dining hall, buzzing noises, clattering trays and rising voices welcomed me and I wondered how I would survive this room without feeling as if my head was on the verge of exploding. I immediately pulled out my headphones, because that was the only way of escape that was left.

For a moment, my eyes shut tight, and I instantly got teleported to a different time and place. The music was a balm to my soul, transporting me to a time when I was happy and not filled with stress and worries, where the fatigue could not touch me. I kept my eyes closed for a few more minutes, the voices in my head began to go quiet, and I wished that it could stay like this forever.

But I knew that the reality would eventually catch up to me. I sat down alone amongst lively clusters, I felt like an outsider and not even a passing glance acknowledged my presence. My mind wandered again, head still throbbing, and the food on my plate was forgotten after a few bites.

I had always been somewhat of a loner, even before my illnesses hit me, I preferred the company of books to people and spent hours curled up on my sofa. My peers always perceived me as a weirdo and I had to face bullying and rejection throughout my whole school years. I always felt different and a lot of older people called me special, but when I was younger, all

I wanted to be was normal, usual, just like everyone else. I could not help but ask myself if anyone else noticed this silent struggle behind my headphones or perhaps if anyone felt the same way as me. My eyes scanned the room and caught the flicker of dimly lit corners, where shadows danced in the quiet spaces. Nausea crept in, and I knew that I would abandon my half-eaten meal any minute now.

I stood up and decided to step outside for the rest of my break. I sought comfort under my tree, away from judgment and the persistent ache within. The time passed quietly, and I listened to the rustle of the leaves and watched the movements of the ducks on the water.

I wondered if my life would look like this forever, ... *would my body always ache with every movement? Is there a life waiting for me with fun and social interactions or am I damned to live in pain and loneliness for the rest of my life? Is living even worth it if I cannot do the things that I love and travel to all the places described in the books that I read?*

I hated the fact that the only way to answer all of these questions was time. All I could do was wait, wait and see how things would turn out. But is a life that is filled with waiting and no real living, even a life?

Chapter 3: reflections in the rain

The rest of my day was spent curled up in bed, buried under endless layers of blankets, avoiding the bustling university halls. Occasionally, a tear rolled down my cheek, and it had left a small wet spot on my pillow right underneath my right eye. My legs felt like they might never move again, and every single muscle in my body ached. I stole a quick glance outside my window, it was storming like crazy. The rain lashed against the glass, the wind howled through the trees and in the distance I could hear the thunder growling. It was scary, yet comforting, like the weather portrayed my feelings within.

My mind wandered to the person I used to be, and I could not help but hate myself for missing out on life because of anxiety. It felt like an unfair burden, even though, deep down, I knew I could not have predicted this reality just a few years earlier. After a while, I stood up and pulled a box out from under my bed. I took a deep breath before I pushed the lid softly to the side. It held memories of my healthier self and childhood pictures with my old friends. Each photograph became a portal to a time when life was less complex and when life was just about living it.

Before heading off to university, I lived in a small cottage a few towns away. Life at home with my parents was anything but simple, our relationship was complicated. Though I knew that they loved me deeply, I often felt misunderstood when it came to my illnesses and the toll it took on me.

I glanced up from the box and took a look around at my dorm room. I never took the time to fully decorate it and it was a complete mess. I owned so much stuff and held onto my past tightly, hesitant to release the threads of my old life and former self, not ready yet to confront the changes that illness had brought. My room was filled with dirty dishes and clothes scattered all over the floor. I felt internal hate for myself, even though I knew deep down that none of this was my fault. The circumstances had woven themselves into my life, leaving me grappling with the aftermath, and now I had to deal with it if I wanted to or not. It was not a choice to make. It was my life.

I picked up my favourite sweater from my floor. It was a cozy, very soft, grandpa sweater, woven with a tapestry of diverse patterns that I bought a couple of years ago in my favourite thrift store. I held it in my hands for a couple of seconds before I slipped the way too oversized piece of clothing over my bony body. I stepped over to my mirror, it reflected not only my appearance but a haunting emptiness. Dark messy hair framed my face marked by exhaustion, and my light blue eyes, which were once vibrant, now held an unmistakable shadow of sadness. I almost could not bear my own reflection.

Chapter 4: the forgotten volumes

The early morning light crept through the curtains, painting soft streaks of warmth across my room. My head was still throbbing, and my eyes were puffy and swollen, but I had no choice other than to go on with my life. It almost felt like a familiar companion, discomfort had become my daily existence.

It was a beautiful Saturday morning and I decided to make my way to the library. I loved to go in the early hours when the ancient library retained its quiet charm. With purposeful steps, I headed towards the library. The golden glow painted the surroundings, casting a calm ambience on the orange leaves. As I approached the entrance, the familiar scent of parchment and old books embraced me.

The library, with its towering shelves adorned with old leather-bound books, was completely empty. The tall arched stained-glass windows allowed slivers of sunlight to filter through, and the soft warmth made me feel at ease. My fingers danced over the spines, each book held an entire world. The love I held for these volumes was much deeper than just the fondness of the words, it was an escape from my world of pain and sorrow. I spent almost all my time in the library reading, or sometimes I would just sit there and stare at the shelves that stretched from floor to ceiling housing an eclectic collection of books, some were bound in old cracked leather and others were wrapped in cloth that was starting to fade.

I settled into a quiet corner and opened my book. Characters became companions, as I started to read, plots a comforting distraction. These books were not just paper and ink, they were my whole life, guiding me through the storm of my own thoughts. As my eyes traced the sentences, I felt the weight of my struggles lift, and even though I was aware of the fact that it would only be momentarily, things felt simpler. The sun continued its dance with the orange leaves outside, yet in this space, time seemed to stand still.

I lifted my gaze from the pages of the book that I held in my hands, gently placed it beside me, and allowed my eyes to wander, absorbing the entirety of the library that surrounded me.

My curiosity led me to the far back of the ancient room, where dusty volumes seemed forgotten by time. It seemed like these books held secrets that were only waiting to be discovered. I reached out and selected one. Its cover was cracked, the old leather-bound was weathered, and the dust stuck to my sweaty fingertips as I glided over the spine. I opened it and a delicate old yellowish paper floated out.

Chapter 5: poetry in the shadows

I picked the old piece of paper up and it revealed a poem.

In shadows grasp, a whispered plight
a battle fought both day and night,
muscles weak, limbs heavy as led,
and all I can do is lay in my bed.
The world outside spins, passes by,
while I dwell in this prison, wondering why,
and all I want is to move by day,
through the pain, I'll find a way.

The words resonated with me, as if the poet had peered into the depths of my thoughts. For the first time ever, I felt seen and like a whole new world could be revealed before me. All the questions that swirled in my mind seemed answerable with the words in front of me. I wondered whose hands had left their mark on these pages? I glared at the book again, which I still held in my left hand. I opened it, and it revealed margins adorned with annotations, like whispers left behind by souls just like me. The discovery of these long-lost words added a new layer to my connection with books, as if I had stumbled upon a hidden realm within the library where I found comfort.

The annotated words spanned a spectrum of emotions, each creating a chorus of voices that echoed through the pages. Each stroke of ink carried a whole life's story, offering a glimpse into the weight of their struggles. I felt a deep need to uncover the identities behind these annotations and read more about their story. I wondered how they navigated the labyrinth of their own existence, and if these words would help navigate mine.

In the quiet library, a new community had emerged from the shadows of the past and the pages had become a canvas over the years, where disparate lives intertwined through shared pain. I stared at the tall bookshelf in front of me and my eyes traced the spines of the books. A curious thought sprouted in my mind. I wondered how many of these books held secret annotations, confessions etched between the lines, just like the one I held in my hands. The urge to uncover the hidden stories within each volume surged within me like a magnetic pull, tempting me to open every book, to reveal the hidden dialogues.

Chapter 6: battered volumes

The library began to fill with the murmur of voices, and a gentle hum permeated the air. I closed the book that I held in my hands, the weight of its confessions lingering in my hands. Words could not describe how the poem had resonated with me, and I felt this unexpected connection to the anonymous writer.

The now crowded library seemed to mirror the voices within the annotated pages, and my heart beat with excitement and the urge to discover more.

The realization that each book could hold untold tales of secret annotations remained in my thoughts, casting a new light on the dusty volumes that surrounded me.

I reached for more books, and I felt like I was driven by a magnetic pull. My mind filled itself with hope. I picked up one book after the other and winced slightly as I lifted the heavy stack of books, yet quickly brushed off my discomfort with a determined smile. Most of the covers were so washed out that I was not able to read the titles and with my burden of books in tow, I made my way to the Librarian.

She was a kind old soul whose warm smile greeted me with familiarity. Our conversations had become a ritual, since I was in the library almost every day. I felt comfortable around her and like she was the only person on campus who even realized that I existed.

She peered at the books in my arms, a hint of concern creasing her brow as she observed their worn condition.

"Are you sure that you want these, dear?", she asked me gently. *"They are quite battered, I think they are going to be tossed out tomorrow, if you want to you can just take them."*

I nodded eagerly, this was a revelation that only fuelled my excitement more.

I made my way outside, the sun shone brightly overhead, casting a golden glow upon the world below. The warmth of the sun sunk deep into my bones and infused me with happiness.

As soon as I reached my dorm room, I pushed my clothes that were scattered all over my floor, away with my feet, and carefully laid out the books on my carpet.

For a moment, I stood still and just stared at the books, marvelling at the wealth of knowledge that lay before me. My hands were trembling as I reached for the first book, I softly blew away the layer of dust and began to turn its pages.

Chapter 7: footnotes of the forgotten

The first page revealed that the book, which I was holding in my quivering hands, was *"Little Women" by Louisa May Alcott*. It greeted me with nostalgia and the words filled me with a sense of warmth. My mind felt silent for a minute before memories flooded it like an unstoppable tide, and the flashbacks took me back to the first time I read this classic that I loved so very dearly.

I read it during a difficult time in my life, when change was relentless. I was chronically ill for a while, but when I read this book, it was 6 months ago that I lost everything. I wasn't able to go to school any more or live my life like a normal teenage girl. Everything slipped through my fingers like grains of sand. My life was filled with numerous hospital visits and doctor's appointments, and these events had taken a toll on my mental health and made the whole thing even more unbearable. And in the midst of my darkest hours, I lost almost everyone I cared about because things got too difficult.

But then, after those months of pain, it was time to change something. I was trying to get my life back with small steps at a time, and through all of this the little women were by my side, page to page, chapter to chapter.

I started to flip through the pages, searching for annotations left behind by mysterious readers who started to become my companions. A fleeting pang of exhaustion washed over me, but I shook it off and my heart started racing with anticipation.

Then, nestled within the pages, I found it: a small piece of paper, its edges worn with age and the paper had turned yellow. It beard a handwritten note and between the pages it was in, on the right-hand side the line

"I am not afraid of storms, for I am learning how to sail my ship" was underlined.

I unfolded the note, while my hands were still shivering, eager to discover the thoughts of the person who had highlighted this quote.

"Amy march is empowering", the text read. *"The way she reflects resilience and determination in the face of adversity in this quote is everything. It definitely inspires me and I feel like it may also inspire other people who deal with mental and/or physical illnesses to embrace their inner strength."*

I felt tears welling up in my eyes again. I have been really sensitive these days, and my heart swelled with gratitude for the connection I felt to this stranger. At that moment, I realized something powerful, the true reason why literature existed: to uplift, to inspire, and to remind us of our own strength and that we are all connected through these worlds within the pages. That we can weather all of our life's fiercest storms, because we are never truly alone.

Chapter 8: whispers of wisdom

I spent the rest of the day reading through all the books and as the sun started to set, in the afternoon, it streamed through my window, casting golden hues across the room. My eyelids dropped with weariness, but I refused to surrender to sleep, I found myself immersed in a symphony of words. The books were scattered all around me, and it felt like they were coming alive, their quotes seemed to be dancing like ethereal wisps in the air.

My dorm room felt like it was overflowing with literary treasures, and the words of Charlotte Brontë whispered softly to me, *"I am no bird; and no net ensnares me: I am a free human being with independent will."* This quote reminded me that my inner spirits remain untamed and resilient, despite the fact that I am feeling trapped by my illnesses and social expectations. I may be confined physically, but my mind remains free.

I delved deeper into the passages, and discovered more and more precious annotations.

I had just opened the book *"To Kill a Mockingbird" by Harper Lee* and after reading the first highlighted passage, I immediately fell in love with her writing and way of thinking.

"You never really understand a person until you consider things from his point of view... until you climb inside of his skin and walk around in it."

Next to this quote was a yellowish sticky note with the words: *"Most of the time I don't feel understood because most people don't have that kind of empathy and most of the time they don't even want to understand. This quote reminds me of the importance of seeing beyond the surface appearance and that we should truly connect with other peoples' experiences more,"* written on it.

With each quote that I read, and each note that I unfolded, I felt a surge of determination, a renewed sense of purpose. From the gentle encouragement of Louisa May Alcott to Charles Dickens' profound reflections.

The melodies from my record player started to intertwine with the symphony of the quotes, and I felt a sense of harmony wash over me. The room, that was once cluttered and chaotic, now exuded an aura of serenity. And at that moment, amidst the swirling echoes of wisdom, I felt like a new version of me was born, ready to face the world with renewed understanding.

Chapter 9: battles woven in time

As I curled up in my bed that night, I started to reflect on the day I spent immersed in annotated books. They made me feel like I belonged in a way. With every note that I read, I felt more and more connected with those who shared my struggles.

But amidst the warmth of connection, questions about my own emotional journey emerged, and they prompted flashbacks to a time when I had just been diagnosed with my illnesses but also to before that. To a time before the endless hospital visits and doctor appointments, and before failed treatments overshadowed my existence.

My life had been a series of battles, each hospital visit and each doctor's appointment drained me both mentally and physically. For a long time, people did not believe me and I felt so lost because deep down I knew that something was not right.

The weight of it all took its toll, weaving a tapestry of anxiety and depression into the fabric of my being, and I felt like no one would ever understand me.

It felt like an eternity before I stumbled upon doctors who truly believed me. I lived in a world where my pain was often dismissed as pure exaggeration and each day was not only a battle against my illness but also against the constant disbelief that surrounded me. It was a relentless struggle to navigate a society that could not comprehend the invisible torment of pain that I went through. Every ache and every throb was met with scepticism, and I often got called dramatic.

When someone finally saw beyond the surface of my symptoms and acknowledged the depth of my struggles, I felt like a little bit of my burdens were lifted. To have my pain validated, and my experiences acknowledged was all I was longing for. But, of course, the scars of disbelief ran deep, leaving me always on edge, forever braced for the next dismissal or invalidation.

It left me with even more loneliness, which was again not born of solitude, but of the crushing weight of never truly feeling understood.

Growing up, I never felt like I belonged, I still felt the weight of invisible scars that had etched themselves under my skin, every time that I tried to fit in, they reminded me that I was different and would never be normal. I constantly felt like an outsider in a world that seemed to belong to everyone else. No matter how hard I tried to blend in, there was always something that set me apart.

Chapter 10: autumn's embrace

The next day was a beautiful Sunday. It greeted me with a warm embrace of autumn sunlight, as if the weather itself was a metaphor for new beginnings. I slightly winced as I pulled on my shoes, the dull ache in my joints were a constant reminder of my body's limitations. Ignoring the discomfort, I straightened up and made my way to the city near the college for the first time ever. It felt like I was stepping into the unknown, and I was making new, hopefully positive, memories.

The walk there was filled with anticipation, each step carrying me to a world waiting to be discovered. I wandered through the cobblestone streets, amidst the rolling hills and lush greenery of the countryside. I noticed that many shops were closed and almost felt a wisp of disappointment.

Suddenly, the air was starting to get infused with the comforting aroma of brewed tea and freshly baked pastries, creating a sense of nostalgia and warmth.

I followed the smell among the maze of buildings, went through a couple of lanes and finally stumbled upon a beautiful little book café with a sign on the outside, adorned with swirling letters that spelt out the name *"Moonlight pages ~ bookcafé"*.

As I entered, the smell of coffee and books wafted through the air, and it felt like a warm hug pulled me in. The interior was furnished with shelves upon shelves of books, their spines as colourful as the rainbow, and sunlight filtered through the windows, casting soft rays that danced upon the wooden floors.

I settled down in a quiet corner and allowed myself to just exist for a moment, feeling a sense of peace washing over me.

I pulled out the book that I had packed earlier. Someone that once meant a lot to me told me that *"the little prince" by Antoine de Saint-Exupéry* had a big impact on them, and I was confused at first because I always believed it to be a children's book, but when I opened it that day for the first time and started reading it I realized that it was far more than a children's book.

"What makes the desert beautiful is that somewhere it hides a well." - this metaphorical quote spoke to me and I have never forgotten it since. There is often hidden beauty and potential for growth, and it resonated with me. Living with a chronic illness can often feel like you are trapped in a desert, with its relentless heat and hard conditions. It represents the constant struggle, pain and limitations. However, the well still

exists, the hope, relief and small victories can make your journey beautiful in its own way. You just have to search a bit to find it.

I ordered a cup of tea and a freshly baked scone, which was still warm, and continued reading the book with its annotated pages. And as I savoured the warmth of my tea and the comfort of my surroundings, I realized that I felt at home for the first time in forever.

Chapter 11: comfort under the stars

The day stretched on endlessly within the comfort of the little café. With each passing hour, I delved deeper into the stories within my books, taking in all the wisdom and hidden worlds.

After a while, a persistent ache nestled within my bones, but I pressed on and tried my best to ignore every bit of it. I was determined to soak in every moment and every little detail of this comfort that I was offered. As the sun dipped below the horizon, painting it in rich colours that reached from amethyst to sapphire, a sense of restlessness stirred within me.

I stepped out into the cold and crisp evening air, grateful for its refreshing touch against my skin. Street lamps were lit at every corner, which cast a warm amber glow upon the streets.

I made my way to my willow tree by the tranquil lake, leaving the small city behind me. The stars twinkled overhead, guiding my path through the amber-leaf carpeted ground, their rustling whispers were a gentle reminder of the changing seasons and that nothing lasts forever. Among the stars was Sirius, the brightest star, who shimmered beautifully like a beacon amidst the celestial tapestry, casting an ethereal glow upon the lake.

I nestled beneath the outstretched branches of the willow tree and allowed myself to breathe, and just exist for a minute, in the presence of something greater than me.

With a soft, almost completely quiet click, I turned on my flashlight, its beam cutting through the darkness with a clarity that almost felt enchanting.

After the last midnight stroll, I changed the batteries, and they proved their worth, casting a warm glow upon the golden brown leaves that were scattered around me.

I could not help but think about the countless nights I had spent in this very spot. So many had been tainted by sadness and pain, by tears shed under this cover of darkness. Whenever I could not sleep because the pain made it impossible to, I sat right here and just stared into the nightfall, listening to the soft rustle of the leaves and the water gently lapping against the shore.

But tonight felt different. Ever since I found the books, the rain had stopped, no sorrow was weighing heavy on my heart and I felt lighter and free.

Charles Dickens' words echoed in the recesses of my mind, *"Suffering has been stronger than all other teaching, and has taught me to understand what your heart used to be. I have been bent and broken, but - I hope - into a better shape"*.

I felt that my mind was making a new memory, a moment of peace that I knew I would treasure for years to come.

Chapter 12: colour in the cold

The air grew colder and stormier every day, and winter was definitely on its way. The new week dawned, and with it, a renewed sense of purpose.

For the first time in what felt like an eternity, I took my time to pick out an outfit that reflected me and my creativity that I had almost lost in this storm. It was a stark contrast to the dullness that had plagued my every being in the last couple of months. It felt nice to look confident on the outside, yet I was still engulfed in a sea of pain. I decided to just ignore it, and resolved to push through.

I was determined to make this work, determined to make something out of my life. I grabbed a couple of painkillers, swallowed them without a second thought, and headed to campus.

As I made my way to the university, the towering spires and stone carvings of the campus loomed overhead. The sound of laughter and chatter filled the campus, and my gaze fixed itself firmly on the ground. I have always remained a silent observer and no one ever seemed to notice me.

Lost in thought, I walked through the cobblestone courtyard. I barely noticed the figure that was

approaching me until they tapped me on my shoulder
and started talking. Their voice was cutting through
the haze of my mind like a ray of sunshine piercing
through the clouds, and I was slightly startled.

*"Hey, I have seen you around before, you are also in profes-
sor William's class, right?"*

The voice belonged to a girl with dirty blonde hair.
Her style seemed to reflect her vibrant personality,
with an array of colours and patterns adorning her
clothes. I definitely noticed her in some of my classes
before, but I could not recall ever hearing her name
before. I was very surprised that somebody actually
noticed me, so I just nodded silently.

*"Well, I just wanted to say that I really admired your in-
sights last week, you always bring a certain unique perspec-
tive to the table"*, she continued, offering me a genuine
smile.

For a moment, I just stared into her deep blue-ish, almost grey eyes, my mind was struggling to process
this unexpected compliment from a stranger. In all
my time at university, no one had taken the time to
acknowledge my contributions, let alone offer praise
for them.

I managed to whisper a little *"thank you"*, my voice
barely audible.

*"No problem, I just wanted to let you know that your voice
matters even if you don't always realize it..., anyways I*

have to go now, but if you want to do something, just hit me up. Oh, and my name is Tara."

With those words she disappeared into her classroom with a sea of students following her, leaving me standing there feeling a strange emotion, a weight I had not even realized I was carrying was lifted, and I thought *"I think this is what happiness feels like."*

Chapter 13: falling apart

——— ⋆·☼·· ⋆ ———

At lunchtime, I made my way to the cafeteria. I intended to sit alone again, just like I had every other day, so far. The solitude had become a sort of comfort that I was clinging to, but today, something compelled me to break the pattern. I looked around for a moment and spotted Tara across the cafeteria, she was laughing with her friends and her extroverted being was lighting up the whole room. She was radiant and full of life. I decided to get over my anxiety and go to her. *"Hey,"* I said, trying to sound casual. *"Mind if I join you?"*

She looked up and her smile widened. *"Of course not! Come sit with us!"*

I took a seat beside her, my anxiety was buzzing in my stomach. They talked about classes and life, and occasionally they asked me questions. Her friends were kind and welcoming, but it was all too much, and I was feeling terribly overstimulated.

The cafeteria was a cacophony of voices and clattering trays. And suddenly the room felt smaller, hotter. I tried my best to focus on Tara and kept telling myself to breathe. The conversation blurred into background noises and my heart started to beat faster. I could feel the rhythm speeding up, each beat more pronounced than the last. I tried to smile and nod, but inside, I felt the panic rising. In the distance, I heard the bells ringing and everyone got up.

I grabbed my trail and did the same, the edges of my vision began to blur, strange dots and colours started to dance before my eyes. I blinked hard a couple of times, hoping to clear it, but that only made it worse, and the colours grew more intense, shapes shifting.

"I think I need to…" I whispered, my voice trailed off as the dizziness hit me like a wave. I reached out, trying to find something to hold on, but my fingers grasped at empty air. The room spun faster and faster and suddenly the colours blended into darkness. I felt myself falling, a brief moment of weightlessness, then nothing.

When I came to, the first thing I heard were muffled sounds, people panicked, and it was a chaos of voices. My eyes fluttered open to see faces hovering above me. I heard someone screaming for help, their voice cutting through the haze.

I felt the cold ground beneath me. Fragments of a shattered plate were scattered around and Tara was sitting beside me. Her hands were trembling, and she was as white as a ghost. I could tell that she was worried. She tried her best to comfort me and kept telling me *"you're okay, help is on the way, you are going to be fine."*

Chapter 14: silent scars

If you had told me the morning of the incident, that it would be the last time for a while that I would leave my dorm room, I would not have believed you. But after that day, everything changed. My body crashed, worse than ever before. The exhaustion hit me like a tidal wave, and I was confined to my bed.

The cuts on my arm from the shattered plates left slight scars, and reminded me of the time that had passed. Winter had settled in, and the world outside my window transformed into a silent, icy landscape.

The first couple of days, Tara came to visit almost every day. She brought homework, books and treats, and her presence felt like a bright spot in the gloom. She tried to keep my spirits up, but I quickly realized that I could not handle it. The concern in her eyes was too much to bear and the effort of pretending I was okay, to spare her the pain, drained what little energy I had left. And over time I realized that she felt the same. She visited me less and less and sometimes would not show up for days at a time.

One cold winter morning, I heard a soft knock at my door. It was Tara, she was standing there with a blank face. Deep down, I already knew what she was going to say.

She hesitated for a moment, then took a deep breath. *"I can't do this any more,"* she said, her voice trembling. *"It's too much. I thought I could handle it, but..."*

Tears welled up in her eyes, and she looked at me with a mixture of sadness, frustration and anger. *"Every time I see you, it breaks my heart. And I know you're trying to be strong, but it's like we're both drowning, and I don't know how to save either of us."*

I felt a pang of guilt and sorrow, but it was quickly overshadowed by the numbness that had become all too familiar. I was used to people leaving when things got tough, so I didn't fight it.

"I understand," I said quietly, avoiding her gaze. *"You should go."*

She looked at me for a long moment, as if hoping I might say something to change her mind. But I could not.

Since then, the days have stretched into an endless loop of agony. I felt trapped inside my own body and my room, every day that passed it felt less likely for me to find a way out. The winter cold crept through the windows, matching the chill that had settled over my spirit. And I hated that the scars on my arm were a constant reminder of that day and of how fragile I am. I felt a bitter tang clung to my tongue and it filled my lungs.

I could not help but think of Sylvia Plath. A couple of years ago I read a few of her things and her words resonated with me, she perfectly captured the essence of what it meant to grapple with deep emotions.

"I don't know what it is like to not have deep emotions," she wrote. *"Even when I feel nothing, I feel it completely."* This quote perfectly described how I felt at this moment. It was as if Sylvia Plath herself reached out to me across time and space, to show me that I am not alone. I felt all of these emotions at once, anger and regret, pain and sorrow.

I thought about Tara often, and about all the people I pushed away over the years. I told myself that I needed time to heal, but deep down I knew that pushing everyone away wouldn't heal me.

Chapter 15: december's fading light

December was here, and the world outside was covered in a pristine blanket of snow, a picture that looked like it was straight from a movie, and it seemed to mock my misery.

I looked outside my window and saw that fellow students were having a snowball fight. Everyone else was feeling good, enjoying their time off school and buzzing with anticipation for Christmas, but I was lying in bed, tears streaming down my face.

The darkness inside me was so consuming that I could not remember the last time I felt the warmth of hope. I was drowning in my own despair, and I realized that even the act of breathing felt like an unbearable burden that I wished would finally end.

I was barely able to walk a couple of steps, the pain and exhaustion made me collapse every time. My legs were trembling, and I felt so much deep hate for myself, because my body was betraying me at every turn. All I could do was lie down on my bed and stare at the ceiling.

The world outside turned into pure imagination. I had been locked up inside for so long that the once familiar streets, bustling with life and colour, now seemed like distant dreams. I could barely remember the scent of fresh rain on pavement or the warmth that tingles through your body whenever someone hugs you.

Days passed in a blur of gray, and the ticking of my clock, which was standing on my overflowing night stand, was my only companion, its relentless rhythm a cruel reminder of time slipping away. The snow outside kept falling, transforming the campus into a winter wonderland, but to me everything just felt cold and meaningless.

The dorms were mostly empty, because the other students left to spend the holidays with their families. I told my parents that I was spending Christmas with friends, because I could not bear the guilt and questions that would arise if they knew the truth. They never really understood what I was going through and repeatedly told me to *"stay strong"* or to *"push through"*. I knew that I was in fact not strong enough and that facing them would feel like a nightmare.

Christmas came and went. I was able to hear the distant sounds of carollers, the laughter of families that went on Christmas walks and the occasional pop of firecrackers. I missed everything terribly, decorating the tree with my family, the warm glow of the fireplace with gently arranged stockings above, and the joy of opening presents picked out and wrapped with love.

My parents sent me a present, filled with my favourite treats, a new chunky sweater and a handwritten letter, which made me cry even harder.

After I put the sweater on, I stared at myself in my mirror. I felt like a ghost, drifting through the remnants of a life I no longer recognized. My reflection was no longer me, hollow-eyed, a shadow of who I once was. The person I used to be seemed so far away, lost in the fog of my illness. Every breath was a struggle, and my body ached in ways I never thought possible.

New Year's Eve arrived, marked by the muted sounds of celebration in the dorms and outside. I laid in my bed, staring at the ceiling. As the clock struck twelve, a burst of fireworks lit up the sky, their vibrant colours a cruel opposite to the emptiness I felt inside.

The new year began without any celebration or happiness from me. I felt lonely. Everyone was celebrating, hugging and kissing their loved ones, and I was alone in my dark, dreary room. I craved human connection, a touch, a voice, I would have taken anything to remind me that I was still alive.

Chapter 16: the weight of january

———— ★·☼·· ★ ————

The new year was here and the once pristine blanket of snow had started to melt, revealing patches of brown grass and muddy walkways. I still had relentless headaches, they were pounding through my skull, and it was impossible for me to read. The once found refuge and comfort was gone and replaced by a constant, throbbing pain that clouded my mind. The books from the library now sat on my desk untouched, and they were starting to collect dust. The only escape that was left was sleep, but with every day that passed it got harder and harder for me to find peace and drift off.

At night, the loneliness felt even more intense. The silence was deafening, broken only by the occasional creaking of the floors, when people would wander down the halls, or by the whisper of the wind outside. I would lie there, staring into the darkness, feeling the weight of my own despair pressing down on me. Tears would silently slip down my cheeks, a bitter testament to my helplessness.

Without the escape of stories and the solace of fictional worlds, I felt trapped in my own reality, and it seemed like the walls were closing in on me, reminding me that there was nowhere out. Questions over questions were haunting me, and they were swirling in my mind like a relentless storm.

"Why am I like this? Why can't I be stronger? Why am I still fighting? What was I made for?"

I felt abandoned not just by other people, but by my own body, by the universe.

I stayed in this place for a long time, trapped by all those questions. I was unable to see past those heavy clouds, and days bled in one another. The weight pressed down on me and even though I was trapped, life around me did not stop, it kept moving. With every day I felt more and more disconnected, as if I had been dropped into a parallel reality where nothing made sense any more.

One morning, I opened my eyes and my dorm room was not cloaked in the usual grey any more. Soft light filtered through the edges of my curtains. I stretched out my hands, towards the cracks of light, letting the light warm my skin. I realized, that the world had not abandoned me, I had turned away from it. And maybe there was a way to turn back to it.

Term was about to start, and the campus was slowly coming back to life. Students returned, filling the once empty dorms with laughter and chatter. I slowly started to open my curtains again, every day a little bit more, and felt a bit of a shift happening. The sun broke through the clouds more frequently, casting warm rays into my room.

I began to notice the sounds of birds chirping outside my window, the songs a faint reminder of life continuing beyond my isolated existence. The world outside my window was changing, and for the first time in months, I felt a glimmer of hope that maybe just maybe I could change too. The snow continued to melt, revealing the Earth beneath raw and ready for renewal.

Spring was starting to blossom and the first flowers were poking through the damp ground and I slowly started to get up again. Every day, I cleaned my room a bit, just enough to sense an order, but never more than my body allowed. I was still resting and sleeping most hours of the day, but the distant sounds of students gave me hope.

Chapter 17: glimmers of spring

——— ⋆·☼·· ⋆ ———

After a while, I felt a sense of purpose and the urge to venture out again, and I felt ready to give the world outside a try. I tied my greasy and knotted hair into a bun and put on the first sweatpants that I spotted on my floor. They were covered in little stains and had some holes along the seams, but I was unconcerned with my appearance because my looks were the least important thing right now. I picked up my long, warm coat and closed my dorm room door behind me.

Stepping outside, I made my way to my willow tree. My legs trembled slightly, a reminder that my body was still weak. I noticed that the field nearby still had some patches of snow. The contrast between the melting snow and the budding flowers mirrored my own internal transformation, the cold retreating as new life began to emerge.

I sat down underneath my willow tree and reached inside my coat pocket and found one of the annotated books. I clutched the worn book to my chest and remembered that the pages of this book, filled with thoughts of kindred spirits, had been my lifeline.

They had become part of me, each of their stories lived inside of me and their struggles mirrored mine. Suddenly, a flicker of movement caught my eye. It was a fox in the snow, its russet fur stark against the white, his eyes sharp and inquisitive, seemed to lock into mine. I did not move a bit, so I would not startle him. The fox paused, its ears twitching as it assessed my presence. For a moment, we simply regarded each other. There was something almost magical about the encounter, a quiet connection that felt like a sign.

After a couple of minutes, it ran away, and I decided to get up as well and discover more of the awakening nature. The ground was soft and spongy from the melting frost. Each breath I took seemed to fill me with renewed hope, and a sense of wonder about the world around me. The air was clear and cold with an earthy scent. The sunlight filtered through the branches above, casting soft patterns on the ground. A sense of peace settled within me and I started to reflect on the past few months and how my life had changed.

I closed my eyes and took a deep breath. The sounds of nature envelop me, the rustling leaves, the distant chirping of birds and the gentle whisper of the wind. It was as if nature was quietly reassuring me that I belonged here, despite my struggles, I was part of this world.

I stood there at the crossword of my past, gazing at my unwritten future, and realized that life could still hold beauty, even in the face of chronic illnesses. It dawned on me that the true strength was not merely about survival, as I once believed, but about embracing the broken pieces, and against all odds, piecing them back together. Despite the imperfections and limitations, there was a resilience within me, a determination to craft a life that, though different from others, was uniquely mine. This journey has shown me that strength can be found in vulnerability, that accepting my illness and acknowledging my limitations did not make me weak, it made me human. I opened my eyes again and looked ahead. The path before me was uncertain, but it was mine to walk.

Acknowledgements

First and foremost, I want to thank my mom for always being there for me and for believing in me even when I doubted myself. Your constant support has been my greatest source of strength. You never left my side and supported me through every challenge, offering your love and encouragement when I needed it most.

To my best friend, Lema, thank you for standing by my side through thick and thin. You have been my rock, especially when things got tough, and I am forever grateful for your friendship.

Thank you to my grandma, for always believing in me and my projects. Your encouragement means the world to me.

A special thank you to Luna Magali for designing the beautiful cover of my book. Your talent and creativity brought my vision to life in the most beautiful way.

I am deeply grateful to everyone who believed in me and supported me through my journey. Your faith in me means the world to me, and I would not be here without you.

Hidden in the Margins marks 18-year-old Magali Elisa Moon's debut. After living with chronic illnesses for a few years now, she noticed a lack of representation for those with similar experiences and was inspired to write her own book. Despite the challenges of writing with limited energy, she was committed to creating a book that resonates with readers who feel overlooked.

Through her writing, Magali hopes to remind readers that their voice matters and that even when faced with doubt, they can achieve remarkable things.

Instagram: Magalicoralie